THE VERY BEST OF FRIENDS

First published in Great Britain in 1990 by
The Bodley Head Children's Books
20 Vauxhall Bridge Road,
London SW1V 2SA

British Library Cataloguing in Publication Data
Wild, Margaret, 1948-
The very best of friends.
I. Title II. Vivas, Julie, 1947-
823 [J]

ISBN 0-370-31435-2

Typeset in 16/18pt Garamond
Produced by Mandarin Offset in Hong Kong

First published in Australia in 1989 by
Margaret Hamilton Books Pty Ltd, NSW

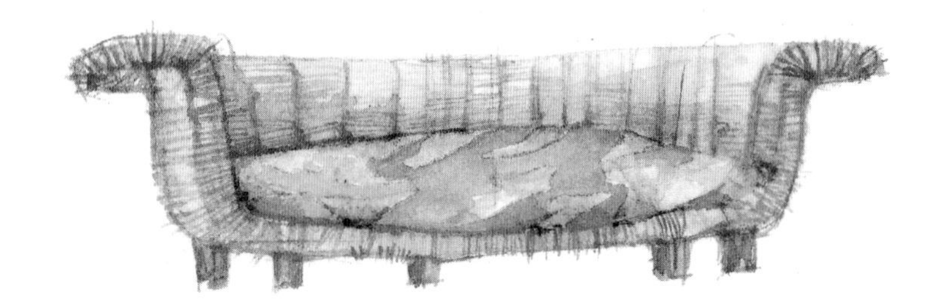

The Very Best of Friends

Margaret Wild and Julie Vivas

The Bodley Head
London

Jessie and James lived on a farm with fifty cattle, twenty chickens, four horses and three dogs. But there was only one cat. William.

James liked cats, but Jessie didn't. "Cats leave hair on the furniture," Jessie said. "Cats are silly, soppy creatures," she said. "Cats aren't nearly as useful as dogs," she said.

Because James loved William so much, Jessie tried to love him too. She always made sure William had a tasty piece of fish and a fresh bowl of milk. She even scratched him under the chin now and again.

But William knew, deep in his heart, that Jessie didn't love him. Not really. Not like James did.

William was careful not to bother Jessie too much. He tried very hard to show her that even cats can be useful.

At the front gate there was an old fridge for a letterbox. Every morning William watched the postman put letters in the freezer, junk mail in the meat tray, telegrams in the butter box and parcels everywhere else.

William miaowed loudly to let Jessie know there was mail. But Jessie didn't seem to understand what he was trying to tell her. She just said crossly, "Stop that dreadful caterwauling! Off with you now. Off!"

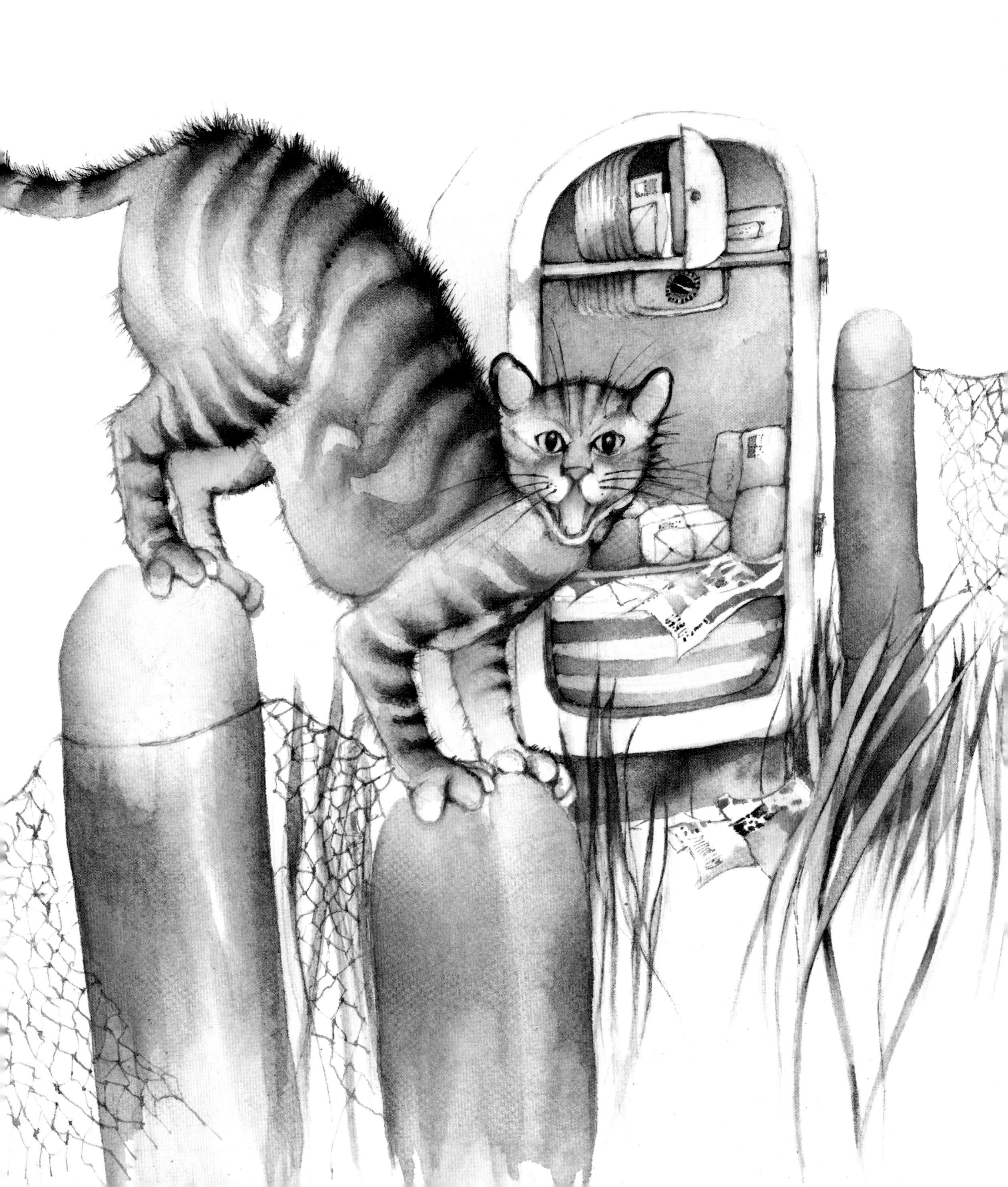

So off William would go. Off to find James.

The two of them were the very best of friends. Together they ploughed the fields and mucked out the stables and dropped bales of hay for the cattle.

But William always made sure he was inside the truck when Boss the bull came near.

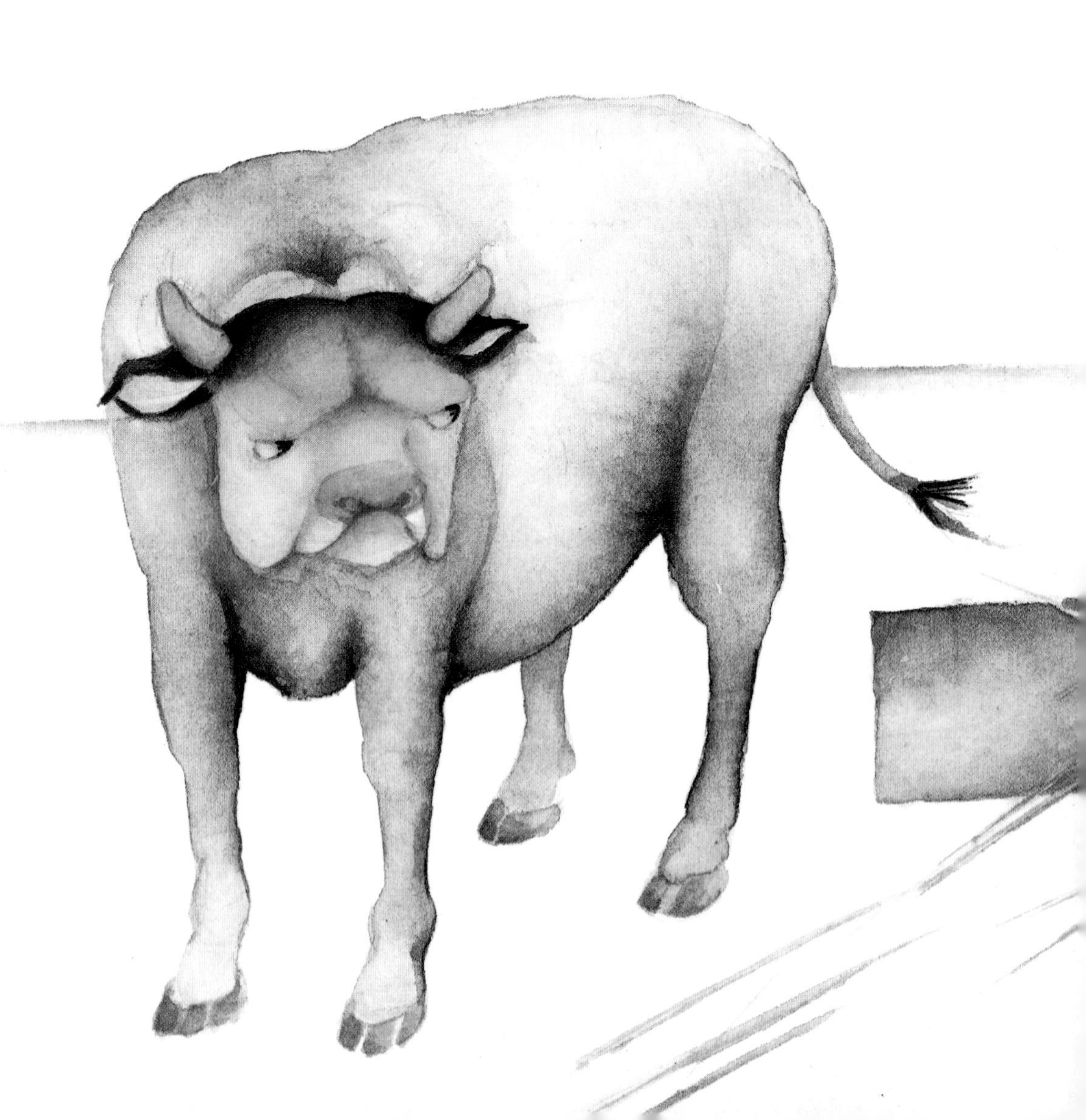

William was very happy inside the house. He had a basket near the fire, two shining food bowls under the kitchen table and a flap in the kitchen door so he could come and go as he pleased.

In the evenings Jessie wrote letters to her one hundred and one pen-friends and James watched TV. William snuggled on James's lap and purred like an engine.

And late at night when Jessie and James were fast asleep, William jumped on to the bed and slept on James's feet. James said he was better than a hot-water bottle, any day.

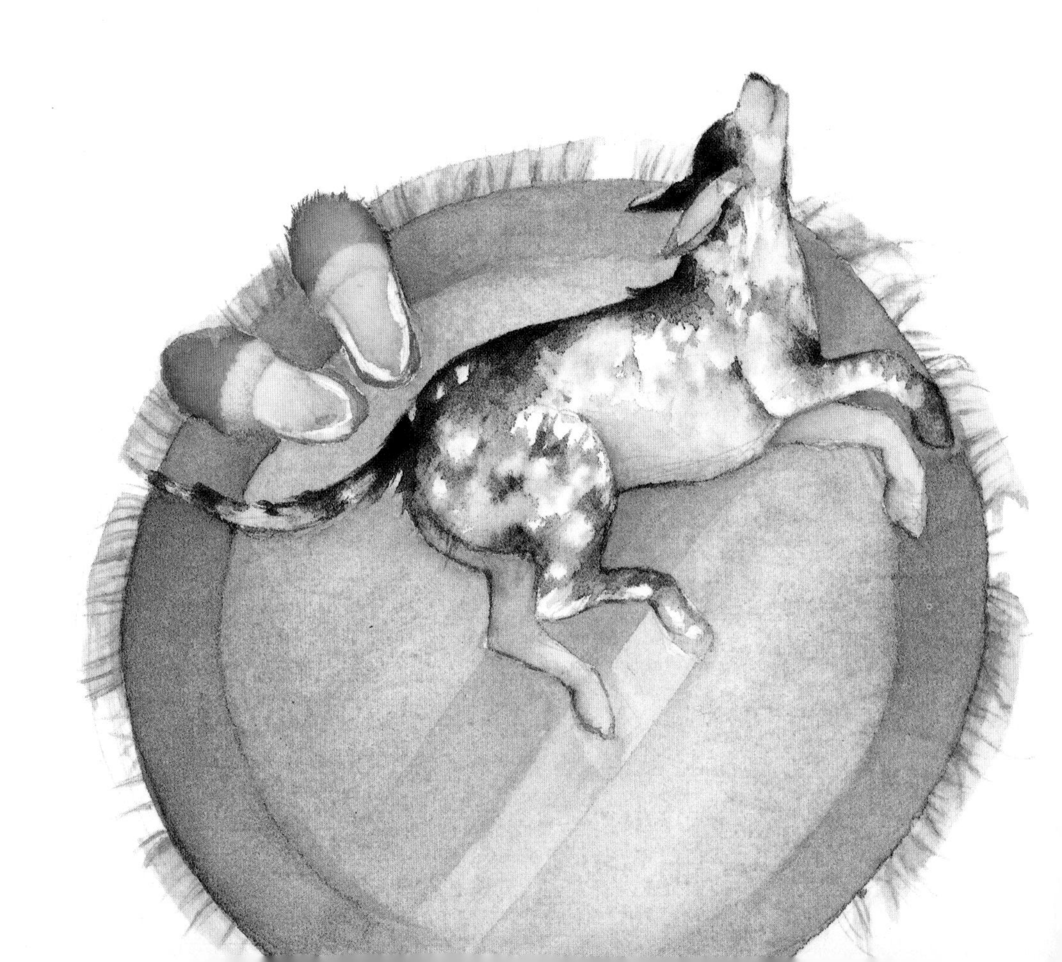

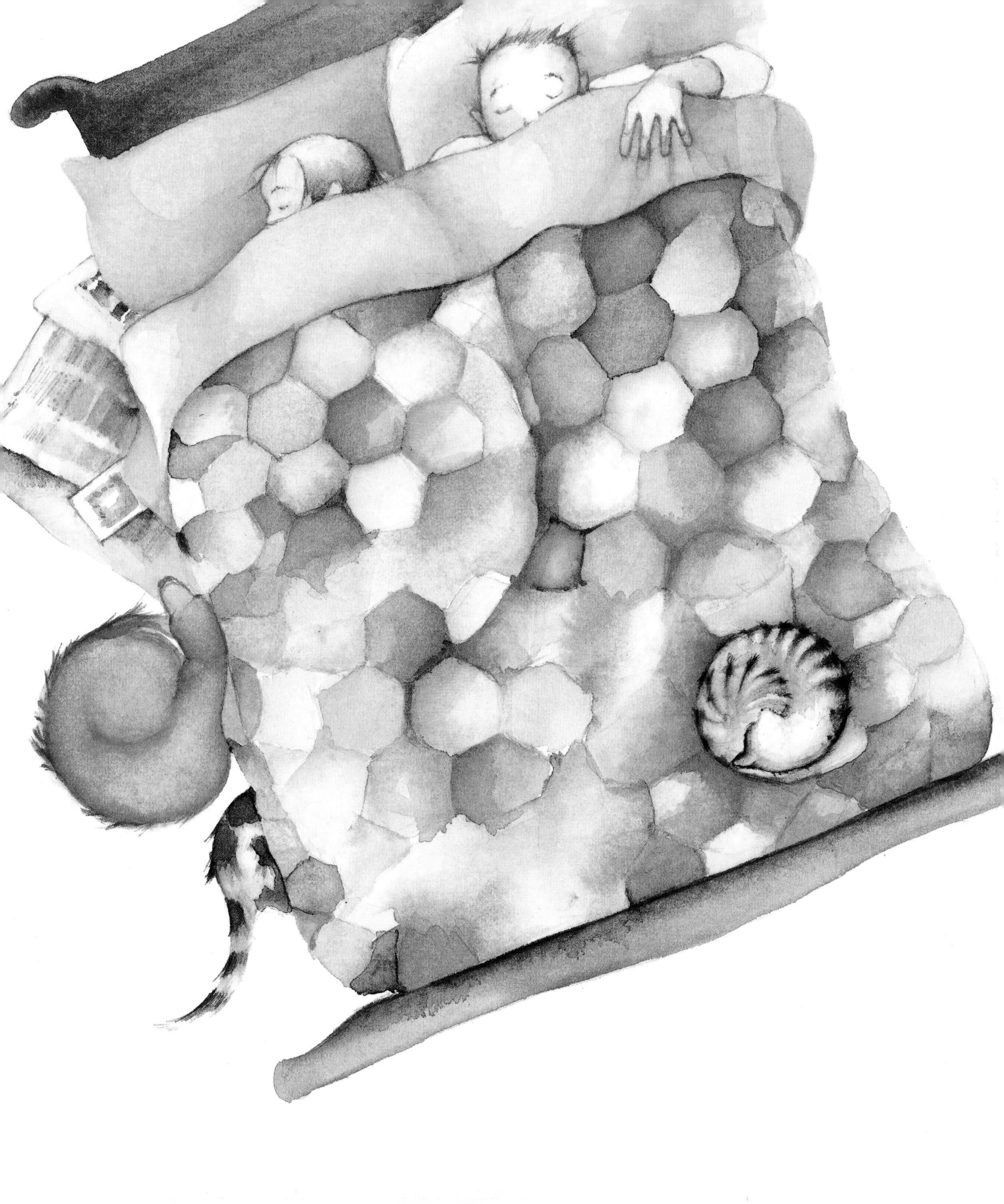

Then one Sunday morning James died, suddenly, of a heart attack.

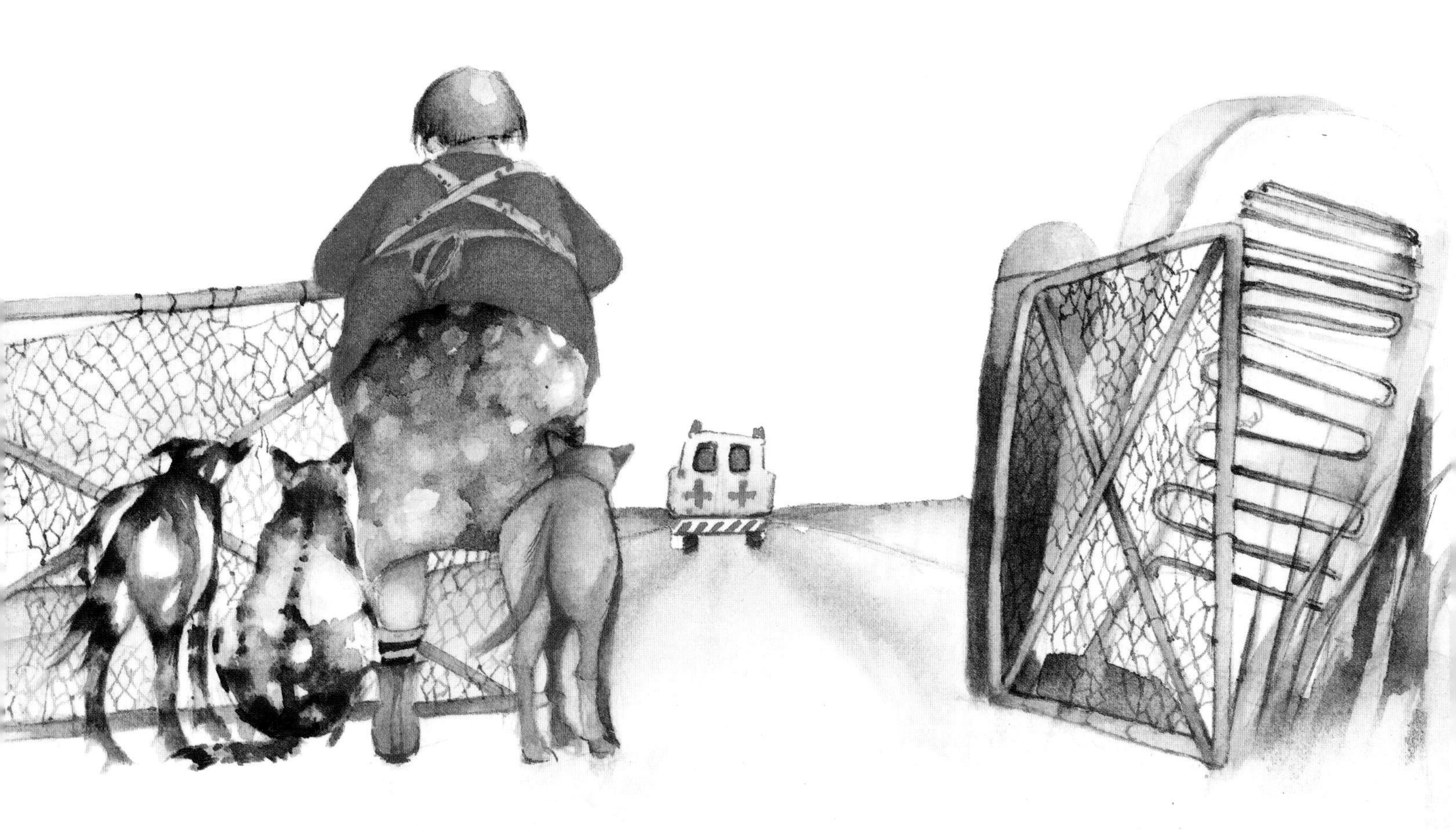

Jessie cried a lot when she thought no one was looking, and William spent his days lying on the bales of hay in the truck, waiting for James to feed the cattle.

Jessie became very quiet and very forgetful. She didn't write any letters and she didn't collect the mail, even though William miaowed extra-loudly. She didn't keep his bowl full of milk and she never scratched him under the chin any more. It was a long time since William had purred like an engine.

He tried rubbing his head against Jessie's legs, but she didn't seem to hear him or see him. Instead, she looked straight ahead and said, "The house smells of cat. I think you should stay outside from now on."

She put William's two food bowls outside the kitchen door and bolted the cat-flap. She put his basket next to the tractor in the shed and said, "From now on you can sleep here. It's warm in the shed and you will soon get used to it."

William didn't like sleeping in the shed. It was dark and lonely. It smelled of paint and petrol and chicken manure.

He didn't like being shut out. He miaowed and yowled and scratched at the door. But Jessie didn't seem to hear him or see him.

Sometimes when she opened the kitchen door, William dived into the house and crouched under the table. There he stayed until Jessie crawled after him and pulled him out and carried him back outside.

So William chased the chickens and swung on the washing and rolled in the vegetable patch. But Jessie didn't seem to hear him or see him.

He tried telling her that the fridge was chock-a-block with mail, but Jessie just closed the windows and drew the curtains and watched TV all day and all night.

After a while William stopped trying to sneak into the house. He stopped miaowing and he stopped watching the postman trying to cram more and more mail into a very full fridge. Instead, he just lay on the bales of hay in the truck and glared at the house with its shut windows and its shut doors.

And late at night William prowled the country roads and fought with cats and hunted anything that moved. He grew mean and lean, and he hated everything and everyone.

One morning when Jessie put out his bowl of leftovers as usual, William hissed at her and scratched her on the hand.

Jessie cried "Ouch!" and sucked her hand. She stared at William. "Why did you do that?" she asked. She stared harder at him. William looked mean and lean. He had a torn ear and a bald patch in his fur. He didn't look a bit like James's cat any more.

Jessie left the kitchen door wide open while she bathed her hand and put on a plaster.

Then she did three things.

First, she unbolted the cat-flap.

Then she brought in William's two grubby food bowls, washed them and put them under the kitchen table.

Last of all, she fetched his basket from the shed and put it near the fire.

"I'm sorry I've been so mean to you," said Jessie, "but I think I'm better now. Will you come into the house with me? We could get to know each other. Perhaps one day we could be the very best of friends."

But William stalked off, eyes flashing, tail in the air. He crouched under the tractor and there he stayed, until Jessie crawled after him and pulled him out and carried him into the house.

So now, in the mornings, William watches the postman put letters in the freezer, junk mail in the meat tray, telegrams in the butter box and parcels everywhere else. He miaows loudly to let Jessie know there is mail. Jessie says he is a very useful cat and always lets him help unwrap the parcels.

Then he and Jessie plough the fields and muck out the stables and drop bales of hay for the cattle. And both of them make sure they are inside the truck when Boss the bull comes near.

In the evenings, while Jessie writes letters, William snuggles beside her and purrs like an engine. He knows, deep in his heart, that Jessie is beginning to love him a lot.